This fairy-tale adventure belongs to

....

LADYBIRD BOOKS

UK | USA | Canada | Ireland | Australia | India | New Zealand | South Africa

Ladybird Books is part of the Penguin Random House group of companies
whose addresses can be found at global.penguinrandomhouse.com.

www.penguin.co.uk   www.puffin.co.uk   www.ladybird.co.uk

Penguin
Random House
UK

First published 2019
001

Printed in China

A CIP catalogue record for this book is available from the British Library

ISBN: 978-0-241-37160-2

All correspondence to:
Ladybird Books
Penguin Random House Children's
80 Strand, London WC2R 0RL

Peppa's Fairy Tale

Once upon a time, Peppa and George were looking at storybooks together.
"This one has three bears, porridge and a hungry wolf looking for an old lady to eat!" said Peppa.

George looked worried.
"Don't worry, George," added Peppa. "There's always a
happy ending." Peppa sighed. "I wish we lived in a fairy story."

"Peppa! George!" called Mummy Pig. "It's time to go to Granny and Grandpa Pig's house for lunch. We're going to walk there through the woods."
"But we want to go on a magical fairy-tale adventure!" said Peppa.

"Maybe if we look hard enough, we might see some magical things on the way," said Daddy Pig.

"This doesn't feel like a magical fairy-tale place,"
said Peppa, as they walked through the woods.
"It feels a bit magical to me," said Daddy Pig,
looking at the trees around them.

"Yes," agreed Mummy Pig. "This is like the path in *Little Red Riding Hood*!"
"I wouldn't be surprised if we bumped into the Big Bad Wolf!" said Daddy Pig. "Ho! Ho! Ho!"

Just then, Daddy Pig bumped straight into Mr Wolf!
"OH! Hello, Mr Wolf," said Daddy Pig. "How are you?"
"Very well," replied Mr Wolf. "I'm just a bit hungry."

"I'm going to my granny's house for lunch," said Peppa.
"Are you really?" asked Mr Wolf. "Well, I'll catch you
later then. Bye!"

"That was just like *Little Red Riding Hood*!" gasped Peppa. "Meeting Mr Wolf in the woods." "I'm not sure which way to go now," mumbled Daddy Pig.
"There's a little cottage over there," said Peppa. "Maybe someone inside will know the way."

Peppa and her family walked through a rose garden and up to the cottage. "Hello?" called Daddy Pig, knocking on the door . . .

As Daddy Pig knocked, the door opened all by itself.
CREEAAAAK!

"Is there anybody home?" asked Mummy Pig, wondering
who would live in a cottage in the middle of the woods.
Inside the cottage there were . . .

three chairs . . .

and three bowls of porridge!

"That porridge looks delicious!" said Daddy Pig. "I wonder whose it is?"

"Hello, Peppa!" cried Belinda Bear, spotting her friend.
"Hello, Belinda!" said Peppa.

"Oh, hello, Mr and Mrs Bear," said Mummy Pig. "Sorry to trouble you, but the door just opened, so we came inside."
"That's quite all right," said Mrs Bear. "It's lovely to see you all!"

"Are you going to stay for lunch, Peppa?" asked Belinda.
"We're having porridge and it's not too hot, not too cold –"
"But just right!" finished Peppa.
"Hee! Hee! Hee!" Belinda and Peppa laughed together.

"We're actually on our way to have lunch at Granny and Grandpa Pig's house," said Mummy Pig. "But we got a bit lost. Could you point us in the right direction, please?"

Mrs Bear pointed the way, and Peppa and her family set off again. "Wow!" said Peppa. "That was just like *Goldilocks and the Three Bears!*"

Hee! Hee! Hee!

"With a little cottage and three chairs," said Daddy Pig.
"And three bowls of delicious porridge . . . I may have
had just a little spoonful!"
"Daddy! Hee! Hee! Hee!" Peppa giggled.
"It's like we are in a fairy tale!"

Peppa, George, Mummy and Daddy Pig followed
the path through the woods to the bottom of a hill.
"I think I need more porridge to get up this hill!"
puffed Daddy Pig.
"Don't worry, Daddy," said Peppa. "We're going
to have lunch soon!"

When they arrived at the house on top of the hill,
Peppa knocked on the door. "Granny! We're here!"

Everyone was very surprised when the
door was opened by . . . Mr Wolf!
"Oh!" they all gasped.
"Oh, hello," said Mr Wolf.

"Mr Wolf!" said Peppa. "Why are **you** here?"
"I'm just round for something to eat," replied Mr Wolf.
"Granny Pig has made a lovely lunch. Mmmmmmmm!"

Granny Pig poked her head around the door.
"Hello, everyone," she said.
"Oh, hello, Granny," said Peppa, a little relieved.
"We're very hungry after all our walking."

"Don't worry, Peppa," said Granny Pig.
"Lunch is ready now."

When Peppa stepped inside, she saw
Wendy Wolf was there, too.
"Hello, Peppa," said Wendy. "What have
you been doing today?"

"Hello, Wendy!" replied Peppa. "We've been having a magical adventure in the fairy-tale woods!"
"Ooooh!" gasped Wendy.

Everyone sat down to eat Granny Pig's delicious lunch.
"Why was it a magical adventure?" asked Wendy.
"It was just like *Goldilocks and the Three Bears* and
Little Red Riding Hood!" said Peppa.

"Wow!" gasped Wendy. "I love fairy stories."
Everyone loved fairy stories.

"Yum, yum!" said Mr Wolf, tucking in.
Everyone **loved** Granny Pig's lunch.

Especially hungry Mr Wolf!